Unicorn
Magic

Slumbertail
and the Sleep Pixies

Daisy Meadows

For lovely Lily Banks

✦ ✦

Special thanks to Elizabeth Galloway

ORCHARD BOOKS

First published in Great Britain in 2020 by The Watts Publishing Group

1 3 5 7 9 10 8 6 4 2

Text copyright © 2020 Working Partners Limited
Illustrations © Orchard Books 2020
Series created by Working Partners Limited

A CIP catalogue record for this book is available from the British Library.

ISBN 978 1 40835 704 0

Printed and bound in Great Britain by Clays Ltd, Elcograf S.p.A.

The paper and board used in this book are made from wood from responsible sources.

Orchard Books
An imprint of Hachette Children's Group
Part of The Watts Publishing Group Limited
Carmelite House
50 Victoria Embankment
London EC4Y 0DZ

An Hachette UK Company
www.hachette.co.uk
www.hachettechildrens.co.uk

Contents

Meet the Characters

Aisha and Emily are best friends from Spellford Village. Aisha loves sports, whilst Emily's favourite thing is science. But what both girls enjoy more than anything is visiting Enchanted Valley and helping their unicorn friends, who live there.

Silvermane

Silvermane and the other Night Sparkle Unicorns make sure night-time is magical. Silvermane's locket helps her take care of the stars.

Dreamspell's magic brings sweet dreams to all the creatures of Enchanted Valley. Without her magical powers, everyone will have nightmares!

Dreamspell

Slumbertail

With the help of her magical friends and the power of her locket, Slumbertail makes sure everyone in Enchanted Valley has a peaceful night's sleep.

Kindly Brighteye is in charge of the moon. The magic of her locket helps its beautiful light to shine each night.

Brighteye

Spellford

Enchanted Valley

Enchanted Cottage

← Golden Palace

An Enchanted Valley lies a twinkle away,
Where beautiful unicorns live, laugh and play
You can visit the mermaids, or go for a ride,
So much fun to be had, but dangers can hide!

Your friends need your help - this is how you know:
A keyring lights up with a magical glow.
Whirled off like a dream, you won't want to leave.
Friendship forever, when you truly believe.

Chapter One
A Sleepless Night

"Aisha?" whispered Emily Turner. "Are you awake?"

The duvet on the bed next to Emily's shifted, and her best friend Aisha Khan's face appeared. By the moonlight shining faintly through the curtains, Emily could see her grin.

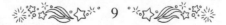

 "I've been
trying to keep
my eyes closed,"
Aisha whispered
back. "But then
I start thinking
about unicorns,
and I'm wide awake again!"

Emily giggled. "Me too!" The two girls
were having a week-long sleepover at
Enchanted Cottage, where Aisha lived
with her parents. They were in Aisha's
bedroom, each snuggled under a cosy
duvet.

"I tried counting sheep, but that didn't
work," Emily said. "So then I tried
counting unicorns. But that just made me

wonder what Queen Aurora was doing!"

Queen Aurora was the unicorn who ruled over Enchanted Valley, a magical world of wonderful creatures – and the girls' special secret. They had been to Enchanted Valley for lots of adventures, and helped save their unicorn friends from a wicked unicorn called Selena. She wanted to rule over the whole land and would do anything to make that happen.

"We're both too awake to sleep now," Aisha said. "I know! Let's have some milk and cookies instead."

The girls got up and put on their fluffy slippers and dressing gowns. Emily went over to the chest of drawers to fetch their matching unicorn keyrings, which were hanging from one of Aisha's athletics trophies. The magical keyrings were gifts from Queen Aurora, so she could call them back to Enchanted Valley. The girls took them everywhere.

Slipping the keyrings into their dressing-gown pockets, they padded quietly down the stairs, careful not to wake Mr and Mrs Khan. In the kitchen, Aisha filled two glasses with ice-cold milk while Emily took a box of hazelnut cookies out from one of the cupboards.

They sat down at the kitchen table. The curtains were open, and the girls gazed out at the velvety black night sky, sprinkled with stars. The moon was a curl of silver. "It's called a waxing crescent

when it's like that," Emily explained. "In about three weeks it'll be a full moon."

Aisha was impressed – but not surprised. Emily was a science whiz! "I wonder if—" she started. Then she gasped. "Emily, look!"

Emily glanced down to where Aisha was pointing – at her dressing-gown pocket. Light shone through the fabric.

Her heart racing, Emily took out her keyring. Aisha pulled out hers too. The crystal unicorns were glowing!

"You know what this means," said Aisha, grinning.

Emily grinned back. "We're going to Enchanted Valley!"

The girls held the keyrings together so the unicorn horns were touching.

Immediately, the kitchen seemed to melt away. A dazzling rainbow of sparkles whooshed around them. They held hands tightly as they were lifted up, up, up …

When their slippers touched the ground again, the girls were no longer in the Khans' kitchen. They were standing on grass, under a night sky. Ahead of them they could just make out a hill where there stood a palace, gleaming faintly gold through the dark.

They were back in Enchanted Valley!

The two girls hurried up the hill. "It looks like Selena's horrible magic hasn't gone away," said Aisha, her slippers rustling through the grass. Selena wanted the throne of Enchanted Valley for herself.

She was responsible for this darkness, and had threatened she would never end it unless the unicorns made her their queen.

They reached the palace. Roses grew up the golden walls, filling the air with their sweet scent. A drawbridge lay across a moat of water, and standing on it was a beautiful unicorn. She glimmered with soft shades of orange, gold and red – all the colours of a beautiful sunrise. She dipped her long, elegant horn in greeting.

"Welcome back, girls," the unicorn said. Her voice was low and sweet, like a cello.

"Queen Aurora!" Emily and Aisha cried together. Aisha threw her arms around Aurora's neck and hugged her. Aurora laughed.

Queen Aurora was followed by another unicorn, who was candyfloss pink with a deep pink mane and tail. Her horn was pink and sparkling. The girls had met her before – she was Slumbertail, one of the four Night Sparkle Unicorns who looked after night-time in Enchanted Valley.

"It's lovely to see you!" said Slumbertail, and the girls hugged her too.

When she pulled away, Emily glanced at Slumbertail's neck. All the unicorns wore a locket that gave them the magic they needed to do their job in Enchanted Valley. Queen Aurora was in charge of friendship, and her locket contained twin suns playing together. But Slumbertail's neck was bare.

"Selena's still got your locket," said Emily in dismay.

Slumbertail nodded sadly. Selena had stolen the Night Sparkle Unicorns' lockets, and was using them to make life horrible in Enchanted Valley. Aisha and Emily had rescued two of the lockets, but they knew the endless night wouldn't be broken until all four were safely back with their owners.

"We'll do our best to find it," Aisha promised Slumbertail.

"We know you will," said Queen Aurora. "But in the meantime, I have decided we must make the best of this darkness." Her eyes shone. "Girls, how would you like to come to a unicorn sleepover?"

Both Emily and Aisha grinned. "We'd love to!"

Chapter Two
The Unicorn Sleepover

Aisha and Emily followed Queen Aurora
and Slumbertail over the drawbridge
and into the golden palace. They walked
through a courtyard dotted with lilac
trees. It was still and quiet, and there were
no lights at the windows.

"I love sleepovers," said Slumbertail, as

they passed a fountain. "Lots of fun with friends, and then I use my magic to send everyone into a beautiful, restful sleep. I can't wait!"

The girls exchanged puzzled glances.

"But Slumbertail, you're the sleep unicorn," said Emily. "If your locket is missing, doesn't that mean you haven't got your magic any more?" She frowned. "How can anyone in Enchanted Valley sleep until we get it back?"

"No sleep!" said Aisha. "That would be horrible."

Slumbertail gave the girls a wink. "Just wait and see!"

They stepped through an archway, crossed another courtyard, then went

through a big pair of wooden doors into
a huge hall. Unlike the rest of the palace,
the hall was brightly lit – and filled with
unicorns!

Soft pillows and blankets covered the
floor. Some of the unicorns were snuggled
up on them, chatting together. One

corner of the hall had been set up as a
little salon with tables and mirrors. There,
a unicorn with ribbons plaited into her
tail nodded her horn, transforming a
little unicorn's straight mane into a spiky,
punky style. Another group of unicorns
were playing board games, and in the
centre of the hall was a table covered
with snacks – crisps, sweets, chocolates,

and popcorn. All the unicorns had cosy
dressing gowns draped over their backs
and some wore fuzzy slippers.

Aisha's eyes were wide. "This is the best
sleepover ever!" she declared.

"Definitely!" agreed Emily, smiling.

Three familiar unicorns got up from
watching a film and came to join them.
Along with Slumbertail, they were the

Night Sparkle Unicorns. "Hi, Emily! Hi, Aisha!" cried Silvermane. The girls had already retrieved Silvermane's locket, which held a tiny shooting star and gave her the magic she needed to look after the stars in Enchanted Valley. Beside her were Dreamspell, who looked after dreams, and Brighteye, who took care of the moon. Emily and Aisha had also found Dreamspell's locket, which contained a dreamy image of friends having fun – but, like Slumbertail, Brighteye was still missing hers.

Aisha and Emily gave them each a hug.

"We're about to do our hair," said Brighteye. "Come and join us!"

"Would you like some snacks?" asked

Dreamspell.

"Yes, please!" said the girls.

It really was the best sleepover ever. The girls piled their plates high with chewy star gummies, creamy chocolates and crunchy crisps.

Then Fancymane, the hairstylist unicorn, gave them both new hairdos.

"I hope you like them," she said, as Emily examined her pink highlights and Aisha admired her new curls. Fancymane tried to stifle a yawn. "Goodness! It must be getting late."

Just then, Slumbertail appeared next to them. "Hey, girls, I've got something special to show you!"

Emily and Aisha exchanged excited glances, and followed the pink unicorn across the hall to a large window. Through the darkness they could just see a tall golden tower at the edge of the palace, with a clock face at the top. Instead of numbers, the clock had two pictures – a sun where the number twelve would usually be, and a moon where ordinary clocks had the number six. It had one hand, which was pointing at the sun.

Emily stared at it curiously. "I've never seen a clock like that before," she said.

"It tells us when it's bedtime," said
Slumbertail. "Even in this endless night,
it knows when bedtime ought to be ...
which is any moment now!"

The girls watched the clock for a few
seconds. Then, suddenly, its hand swung
from the sun to the moon. Instantly,
tinkling chimes rang out and a door
beneath the clock face swung open. Out
flew several tiny creatures. At first the

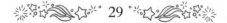

girls thought they must be butterflies, but when the creatures flew closer to the window they saw that they were pixies! Each had silvery wings and lavender-coloured skin, and wore a bright pair of pyjamas and matching nightcap. Their pointy ears poked out from under their caps. The girls gasped with amazement.

"Wow!" said Aisha. "Who are they?"

"My helpers," said Slumbertail proudly. "The sleep pixies!"

The tiny creatures whizzed past the window. They were carrying miniature pillowcases, and when one of the sleep pixies almost dropped his, a shimmering powder spilled out.

"What's that?" wondered Emily.

"Sleepy dust," explained Slumbertail. "I use the magic from my locket to make it. Every night, when the clock says bedtime, the sleep pixies fly across Enchanted Valley and sprinkle the dust over everyone to help them fall asleep."

"We've never noticed the sleep pixies before!" said Aisha.

"They stay high up when they sprinkle their dust," explained Slumbertail.

"Usually everyone drifts off into a peaceful sleep without even noticing the sleep pixies have visited."

"Thank goodness Slumbertail had made a big batch of sleepy dust before Selena stole her locket!" said Queen Aurora, appearing behind them.

All of the sleep pixies flew off in different directions, clutching their pillowcases – except one. She landed on the window frame, and tapped the glass. Her purple eyes were large, and curly purple hair spilled out from under her nightcap. Emily hurried to open the window, and the sleep pixie flew into the room, her wings fluttering as fast as a hummingbird's. "Sweet snoozes to you!"

she said in a voice
as soft as a lullaby.
She stuck out her
tiny hand. "My
name's Trixie!"

Chapter Three
Sleepy Dust

Aisha and Emily both offered Trixie
a finger to shake, and introduced
themselves.

"It's lovely to meet you," Trixie said.
"I've heard all about your adventures in
the valley. Now, watch this!" She scooped
some sleepy dust from her pillowcase and

tossed it high into the air. For a moment it hung there, like a glittering golden cloud. Trixie sang very sweetly:

"The moon is bright
So say good night,
And now sleep tight
Till morning's light."

Both girls sighed happily – Trixie's singing was so soft and lovely. "I just hope the lullaby comes true and it's light in Enchanted Valley again soon," Emily murmured to Aisha.

The dust floated down over the unicorns who were playing board games. One of them, a little black foal, sneezed when some of it landed on his nose.

Trixie carried on sprinkling the

sleepy dust until it had landed on all the
unicorns and the girls. There was even
some sparkling in Queen Aurora's mane.

"In a few minutes, everyone should fall
asleep," said Slumbertail.

Trixie perched on Emily's shoulder
to wait. "Are you feeling sleepy?" she
whispered.

Emily and Aisha shared a look. Neither
of them felt very sleepy.

"Maybe a little?" said Emily, not

wanting to upset the pixie.

The girls watched the unicorns. But no one was closing their eyes.

"Everyone should be nodding off by now," Slumbertail said, with a worried toss of her horn.

Trixie anxiously clutched her empty pillowcase. Queen Aurora's brow was furrowed.

Tap, tap, tap ... Aisha turned around to see another sleep pixie at the window, knocking to be let in. She hurried to open it, and he fluttered inside. He was carrying an empty pillowcase and his little lavender face was scrunched up with worry.

"What is it, Dixie?" Slumbertail asked him.

"The sleepy dust isn't working!" Dixie cried. "All the other sleep pixies are saying the same thing. We've sprinkled all our dust, but everyone in Enchanted Valley is still wide awake!"

Slumbertail gave a whinny of dismay.

"Oh, goodness. No one is falling asleep here, either," said Aurora.

Emily and Aisha glanced around the room of tired-looking unicorns. "But why isn't it working?" wondered Emily.

"Maybe—"

She stopped with a gasp as, outside the window, a fork of lightning cut through the inky black night. There was a rumble of thunder, and the hall filled with shouts of alarm.

"Look out!" cried Trixie.

At the window appeared a silver unicorn. Her mane and tail were twilight blue, and her horn was very long and sharp. She gave an evil grin.

"It's Selena!" cried Aisha and Emily at once.

Selena thrust her horn forwards, and the window shattered with a crash. The unicorns whinnied in alarm. Trixie and Dixie the sleep pixies flew, trembling, to

hide behind the girls.

"Get back, everyone!" cried Queen
Aurora.

Selena flew through the broken
window and landed before them. Flashes
of lightning rippled up and down her
horn, and she stomped the floor with her
hooves. A brown owl swooped in after
her and gave a mocking hoot — it was

Screech, Selena's horrible helper.

Queen Aurora drew herself up. "You are forbidden from the palace, Selena!" she said sternly. "You and your evil magic are not welcome here."

Selena smirked. "I thought you were supposed to be the friendship unicorn. That wasn't very friendly, was it?" Her gaze flickered around the hall. "But it doesn't matter. This palace will soon be mine. Then *you* won't be welcome!"

Screech hooted with laughter. "Good

 one, your nastiness!"

Aisha clenched her fists. "Get lost,

Selena!" she said bravely.

Selena turned her attention to the girls. "I might have known you two would be here," she said. "I'm sick of your interfering ways! But you won't stop me this time."

"We will," said Emily, hoping she sounded more certain than she felt. "Give back Slumbertail's locket!"

Selena tossed her head and cackled. "The locket is mine, and you won't get it back – not unless you agree to make me queen!"

"That will never happen," said Aurora.

"Then say goodbye to the locket for ever," Selena said. She narrowed her eyes. "You meddlesome girls stole the last

locket from me while I was asleep, so this time I will be staying wide awake. And so will everyone else!"

Slumbertail gasped. "So that's why no one's falling asleep — you've stopped the sleepy dust from working!"

"That's right," said Selena. "I've twisted the magic of the locket so no one in Enchanted Valley will ever sleep again, no matter how much of that silly dust you throw around. You'll be too exhausted to stop me from becoming queen!"

She cackled and flew back through the shattered window. Another rumble of thunder made the hall shake.

"Night, everyone!" Screech taunted them. "Sleep well! Oh, wait — no you won't! Ha!" He flapped away after his mistress.

"Oh no!" cried Slumbertail. She dipped her horn low in despair.

Trixie and Dixie emerged from behind the girls. "No more sleep," said Trixie in a horrified voice. "No more snuggling on soft blankets and nodding off!"

Panic spread around the hall. "We'll be too tired to do anything!" cried the unicorn with the spiky mane.

"We won't be able to make food, or tend the flowers, or look after any of the other creatures in the valley!" a red unicorn cried.

The little black foal gave a sob. He still had sleepy dust on his nose. "But I'm so

tired already," he said, his eyes brimming with tears. "I wish I could go to sleep!"

Queen Aurora turned to Emily and Aisha. "Girls, this is terrible." Her tail twitched with worry. "Without sleep, we won't just be too tired to stop Selena – Enchanted Valley will fall apart!"

Emily glanced at Aisha. They knew what they had to do.

"We'll stop Selena," Aisha said. "And we'll get the locket back. We promise!"

Chapter Four
Hob's Potion

"The other pixies will be wondering
what's going on," said Dixie, adjusting
his nightcap. "I'd better go and tell them."
He zoomed away through the broken
window.

Emily rested her chin on her clasped
hands, thinking hard. "Do you remember

when Selena gave Wintertail the Winter Unicorn a potion to make her sleep?" she asked. "Maybe we could make one. That way everyone can have a nap, at least."

"Oh, yes!" cried Slumbertail. "If the unicorns are rested, they'll be able to take care of Enchanted Valley while we search for my locket."

Aisha's eyes shone. "Nice idea, Emily! I bet Hob could help us." Hob was a very old, very clever goblin, who knew how to make all kinds of potions. "Let's go and ask him."

Everyone agreed this was a good plan.

"I'm coming with you," insisted Slumbertail.

"And me," said Trixie. She put her hands

on her tiny hips. "We
must turn this nasty
nightmare into a nice
nap!"

Queen Aurora needed
to stay at the palace, to
guard it in case Selena
returned. "Be careful," she said. "Selena
and Screech will try to stop you. And
good luck!"

As soon as the girls were sitting on
her back, Slumbertail took off and flew
through the broken window, Trixie
fluttering beside her. They soared up into
the night sky. A thrill fizzed through the
girls. Even though they'd had many rides
on their unicorn friends, shooting through

the air was still as exciting as the first
time they'd done it. They couldn't help
beaming with delight as they looked
down to see the palace already shrinking
into the distance.

Slumbertail flew lower than usual, using
the light glowing from cottage windows
below to guide her way. Looking
down, the girls saw that even though
it was dark, lots of creatures were out.

Flowerdew Garden was bustling with gnomes.

"I'm going to dig and dig and dig until it sends me to sleep," they heard a gnome wearing a dandelion cap say.

A gnome in a poppy cap rubbed her eyes. "I'm so tired I can't think straight," she said with a groan. "Was I going to mow the roses or prune the grass?"

Slumbertail flew on. They passed nests

of birds
trying to sing
themselves
to sleep, and
when they
went over one
of the rivers
that wound

through the valley, they saw mermaids
having swimming races.

"Everyone's trying to wear themselves
out," said Slumbertail in dismay. "But it
won't do any good – until we find the
locket, no one will be able to sleep no
matter how tired they are."

In the distance were three large shapes,
flying in circles.

"They don't look like unicorns,"
said Trixie. She gave a squeal. "Biting
bedbugs! They're not Selena's helpers too,
are they?"

Aisha peered at the flying creatures.
They were moving so slowly it was
obvious they were exhausted too. She
could make out jagged wings, pointed
tails and snouts with smoke coming out
of them. "Don't worry, Trixie," she said.
"It's just the dragons from Firework
Mountain." The girls had met the

dragons on their first ever adventure to Enchanted Valley and knew that they were very friendly.

Slumbertail landed in front of the cave where Hob the goblin lived. The girls climbed down on to the mossy ground, and Emily knocked on the stone door. They could hear shuffling noises inside, and then it swung open.

In the doorway stood a little creature with wrinkly green skin. He was half as tall as the girls, and wore a dressing gown decorated with moons and suns. He was cleaning his spectacles on one sleeve.

"*Yaaaaaaaaaawwwn!* Oh, excuse me, so tired ..." He put his glasses back on. "Bless my stars, it's Emily and Aisha! And

Slumbertail! And you must be one of the
sleep pixies."

"Hi, Hob!" said the girls, hugging him.
"This is Trixie."

"You all look very worried, my dears,"
Hob said, gazing around at them. "Why
don't you come in and tell me about it,
and I'll do my best to help."

They followed him through the cave
and into a long tunnel that led to several
spacious rooms. Aisha caught Emily's

eye and grinned – they always enjoyed visiting Hob's house. In his cosy kitchen, the girls sank into armchairs, while Slumbertail settled on the rug and Trixie perched on a bookcase. As Hob heated a saucepan of hot chocolate over the fire, they quickly explained what had happened – about Selena and the stolen locket, the sleepy dust that wouldn't work, and their idea about a potion.

Hob poured the hot chocolate into a bowl for Slumbertail, mugs for the girls and a thimble for Trixie. "A – *yaaaaaaaaaawwwn!* – commotion?" said Hob.

"Oh, no, a potion," said Emily.

"And Selena has stolen the sleepy

dust?" asked Hob in confusion.

Aisha shook her head. "She's stolen Slumbertail's locket."

Hob took off his glasses and rubbed his eyes. "Ah, of course. I'm sorry, my dears, I'm so tired I can't concentrate properly."

"It's not your fault," said Aisha.

Trixie put down her thimble. "You can still make us a sleepy potion, though, can't you?" she asked in a worried voice.

"I shall certainly try," said Hob. "Anything to stop Selena!" He shuffled out of the kitchen. The girls could hear clinking, clanking and several enormous yawns, and then Hob returned with his arms filled with bottles and jars. He set them on the table and gathered bowls,

spoons and a pestle and mortar.

They all clustered around the table to help. Hob asked Emily to grind up some yellow Dreamweed Seeds with the pestle and mortar, while Aisha stirred Lullaby Liquid with Dozy Drops to make a thick orange syrup. Slumbertail cracked Night Nuts on the floor with her hooves, and Trixie retrieved the kernels and dropped them into a bowl of green Snooze Jelly. Finally, Hob used his magical wooden spoon to mix everything together into a bright blue potion. He poured it

into a glass bottle.

"Ta-dah!" he said. "Who would –
yaaaaaaaaawwwn! – like to try it?"

"I will," said Trixie eagerly, fetching the
thimble.

Emily filled it with potion. As the little
pixie took a sip, the girls held their breath.
Would it work?

Chapter Five
Dragon Crash!

"Do you feel sleepy, Trixie?" asked Slumbertail. They were all watching her closely.

Trixie shook her head. She gave a puzzled frown. "But I do feel strange …" Suddenly, she bounced up into the air like a spring. She landed on a pile of pots

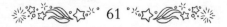

and pans, and immediately bounced up
again. "Eeek!" she squealed, and landed

on Slumbertail's
nose. Then she slid
down, into Aisha's
waiting hand.

"Oh, crumpets!"
Hob cried. He
picked up the
ingredients. "This
isn't Lullaby Liquid – it's Jumping Juice!
And these are Bouncing Beans, not
Dreamweed Seeds …" He groaned in
dismay. "I didn't make a sleepy potion – I
made a *leapy* potion! If only I wasn't so
tired … I'm very sorry, Trixie!"

Trixie shook out her wings. "Don't

worry, it was fun!"

Hob slumped in his rocking chair. "I'm so sorry," he said sadly. "I don't think I can – *yaaaaaaaaawwwn!* – help you after all."

"Please don't feel bad, Hob," said Aisha. "We'll just—" She broke off, as the floor began to tremble. Suddenly, everything was shaking. Books fell from shelves. Hob's mug of hot chocolate fell on the rug, and the potion ingredients rained down on to the floor.

"What's happening?" cried Slumbertail.

Emily grabbed hold of a chair to steady herself. "It feels like an earthquake!"

"An earthquake?" cried Slumbertail. Her hooves skittered on the trembling

floor. "In Enchanted Valley? But there's never been one before!"

Trixie flew around the kitchen in panicky loops. "Dancing duvets!" she squealed. "This is terrible!"

Aisha caught the two bottles of potion before they could fall off the table, and tucked them in her dressing-gown pockets. "There's only one way to find out what's happening," she said. "Let's go outside!"

The friends hurried out of the kitchen and along the tunnel, bumping into the shaking walls. They rushed out of the cave door into the endless night – and gasped. In the branches of the tree that grew above Hob's cave were the dragons!

One was gold, one silver and one bronze.
All three were blinking sleepily.

"Stinging nettles!" cried Hob. "What
are you three doing up there?" He was so
shocked, he wasn't yawning any more.

"We're so sorry," rumbled the silver
dragon, who was called Smoky.

The gold dragon, whose name was
Sparky, nodded his big scaly head. "But
we were so tired ..."

"… we couldn't fly straight," finished Coal, the bronze dragon, "and we crashed into Hob's tree!"

The branches creaked and groaned under their weight.

"No wonder we thought there was an earthquake," said Aisha. "You'd better come down before the tree topples over!"

The dragons flew down to the ground. "If only we could sleep," grumbled Coal. He yawned, blowing out a big puff of smoke.

"I'm afraid none of us will sleep until we find my locket," said Slumbertail.

The dragons looked at each other. "Oh, yes! That's why we were flying here!" said Smoky.

 66

"We saw Selena!" said Sparky.

"She's so mean!" Smoky added.

"She stole our pillows!" said Coal.

Trixie tilted her head. "But what would horrible Selena want with slumbery soft pillows?" she wondered. "She probably likes to sleep on slabs of cold stone."

"They weren't just any pillows," said Sparky, covering a yawn with his gold tail. "They were filled with Feather Flowers!"

Trixie gasped. "Those are the softest, sleepiest pillows in all of Enchanted Valley!" she cried. "No wonder you're cross!"

"We are," agreed Coal. "Or we would be, if we weren't so tired."

"Where did you see Selena?" asked Emily.

"In the mountains," said Sparky. "Are you going to find her? She's so scary!"

Aisha tightened the belt of her dressing gown. "We're going to try," she said. "We'd do anything to save Enchanted Valley. Right, Emily?"

"Right," said Emily.

"Right," Slumbertail said.

"Right," said Trixie. "Stealing lockets *and* Feather Flower pillows? We can't let Selena get away with it!"

Hob gave them each a hug. "In that case, good – *yaaaaaaaaawwwn!* – luck, my dears!"

Chapter Six
The Pillow Fort

The air above the mountains was chilly. Aisha and Emily huddled together on Slumbertail's back, pulling their dressing gowns tight around themselves. In the dark it was hard to see much at all, except the jagged peaks jutting into the sky.

Aisha scanned the steep, empty slopes.

"Nothing," she said with a sigh.

"Maybe the dragons made a mistake, and Selena wasn't here," said Emily.

Slumbertail flew over more rocks and boulders. "I can't see anything either," she said. "I'm afraid this is hopeless, girls. Let's turn back. But where's Trixie?"

Aisha and Emily looked around. "Trixie!" they both called. "Trixie, where are you?"

"Down here!" Trixie's lullaby voice floated up to them. Slumbertail followed it down to a heap of dull grey boulders. Fluttering above them was Trixie, her lavender face lit up in a grin. "Look what I've found!"

The girls' gazes followed Trixie's tiny,

pointing finger. Lying between two boulders was a glittering silver flower, with long, soft petals shaped like feathers.

Emily gasped. "Is that a Feather Flower?" she asked. "From the dragons' pillows?"

Trixie whizzed around in excitement. "It is!"

"Selena might have been here after all!" cried Aisha.

Hope fluttered inside the girls as Slumbertail skimmed over the mountains.

"There's another one!" called Emily, pointing to a shimmery pink Feather Flower lying on the stony ground.

"There's one here, too!" Slumbertail said, flying past a pale blue Feather Flower caught in a scrubby bush.

The trail of Feather Flowers led them up to the top of a mountain peak, where a lilac flower shimmered in the snow, and down the other side. The dark mountains stretched out before them, but closer by something huge and white loomed on the steep slope.

"That's odd," said Aisha. "It looks like a cloud."

But when they flew nearer, they saw it wasn't a cloud at all. It was a big white castle!

"Do you see what it's made of?" asked Emily.

"Pillows!" cried Aisha.

She was right. The walls of the castle were built from stacks of fluffy pillows. Little pillows made up the battlements.

Trixie's eyes were huge with amazement. "It's the biggest pillow fort I've ever seen!" she said.

"The dragons' pillows must be part of the fort," said Slumbertail.

Aisha nodded. "And if Selena stole the pillows …"

"… this fort has to be hers," finished Emily. "She might be here now, with the locket!"

Slumbertail landed on the stony ground, and the girls jumped down from her back. Moving from boulder to boulder, careful to stay out of sight, they all crept closer to the pillow fort. There was an archway that led into the fort, made from several pillows as large as Slumbertail. Standing

outside it were
two big trolls.
They had
warty orange
skin and messy
tufts of hair.
One of them
was wearing
pyjamas and
the other was

in a nightdress. The girls, Slumbertail and
Trixie ducked behind a large rock to
watch.

The troll wearing a nightdress scratched
her armpit. "This isn't fair, Stinker," she
grumbled. "We've been on guard for ages
now. All I want is a nice mug of cocoa

and a sleep. Is that too much to ask?"

Stinker yawned, showing rows of rotten teeth. "Quite right, Surly," he agreed. "This isn't what we signed up for." He waved a hand at the fort. "All these pillows, and she won't let us sleep! Not even one wink!"

"What's all this complaining I can hear?" a voice boomed from inside the pillow fort.

Emily and Aisha shared a glance. They'd know that cruel voice anywhere …

Sure enough, out of the archway strode Selena. Lightning flashed around her horn and her eyes were narrowed with annoyance. Flying at her shoulder was

Screech the
owl.

Surly and
Stinker
immediately
saluted her.

"Talking
about me, were you?" Selena asked the
trolls icily.

"No, your nastiness," said Surly. "Well,
yes, maybe a bit. We were just wondering
if we could have a rest now."

"We've been working really hard,"
added Stinker. "Honest."

Selena stamped a hoof. "How many
times must I explain?" she shouted.
"You two guard the pillow fort, while

Screech and I guard the locket. If I hear any more complaining, you will have no more yucky cocoa, no more silly bedtime stories, and no more sleep! Ever! Understand?"

"Y-yes, your horribleness," stammered the trolls.

Selena marched back inside.

"Have a nice night!" sniggered Screech, and swooped inside after her.

Crouching behind the rock, the four friends leaned close together to work out what to do.

"I feel a bit sorry for those trolls,"

whispered Emily. "But we need to get past them somehow."

Aisha nodded. "If we could just distract their attention from the archway …" she said.

Trixie grinned. "I've got an idea!"

Keeping away from Surly and Stinker, she whizzed up to the top of the battlements and grabbed one of the small pillows. Then she floated down, holding on to the pillow, until she was right above the trolls. Surly was yawning while Stinker picked his nose. Suddenly, Trixie darted down and – *whumph!* – bumped Stinker on the back of his head with the pillow.

"Oi!" cried Stinker, turning to Surly.

"What did you do that for?"

"Do what for?" asked Surly.

"Someone hit me!" Stinker grumbled.

Both trolls looked around, scratching their tufty heads. Trixie zoomed down again, and this time hit Surly with the pillow. *Whumph!*

"Hey!" Surly whirled around. "Someone's playing a prank on us, Stinker!"

The trolls began searching the area

around the pillow fort, peering through the darkness to check behind rocks and under the prickly bushes.

Trixie raced back over to rejoin Slumbertail and the girls.

"That was brilliant, Trixie!" whispered Aisha. "Come on, before they see us!"

While Surly and Stinker were bent over, searching a knobbly tree, the friends crouched low and ran through the darkness, towards the archway that led into the pillow fort. The girls' hearts were racing. Would they make it in time? The fort was getting closer … and closer …

"Nearly there," panted Emily.

But Stinker gave a shriek. "Intruders!" he yelled. "I've found them, Surly!"

Emily and Aisha looked back in horror.
The trolls were pounding towards them!

Chapter Seven
A Big Leap

Slumbertail galloped in front of the girls and halted, her hooves skidding on the rocky ground. "You go on ahead, girls," she told them, picking up a pillow. "I'll hold off Stinker and Surly!"

"Oh, thank you!" cried the girls.

"I'll help!" added Trixie. She hovered

next to Slumbertail, her tiny hands on her hips. "I'm not scared of any troll!"

Aisha grabbed Emily's hand and used her extra speed to pull her along, sprinting for the archway. They burst into the pillow fort, panting for breath.

It was like being inside a cloud. Everything was soft and white – the walls, the ceiling, even the floor. The girls caught their breath and listened. An excited, high-pitched squawk was coming from somewhere within the fort.

"Screech," whispered Emily, and Aisha nodded.

Still holding hands, the girls made their way towards him. Doing their best not to stumble on the pillow floor, they tiptoed down a corridor made of pillows, hurried through a pillow hallway, and peeked around a corner into a pillow room.

Screech was swooping from one end to the other, then back again. "Night-time is the best time!" he yelled. "No horrible sunshine! Just lovely darkness! Don't you agree, Selena?"

Selena was sitting in a corner, her legs tucked underneath her, scowling. "Will you be quiet, Screech?" she snapped. "I'm actually getting bored with this endless night, but it's necessary to make sure those girls are too tired to find the locket."

Screech fluttered in front of her. "But the dark is fun, Selena—"

"I SAID BE QUIET!" Selena shouted, then yawned loudly.

Emily caught Aisha's eye. Selena was obviously as exhausted as everyone else in Enchanted Valley.

Screech dropped down on to the pillow floor. He put a wing over his beak. "Won't say another word," he said. "Promise!"

Something glinted against his feathery chest. Aisha stifled a gasp and gave Emily a nudge. Hanging from Screech's neck was a pendant containing a tiny pillow spinning round and round. Slumbertail's locket!

Selena yawned again. "It's a good thing

you're not tired, Screech," she said. "It means you can guard the locket. Otherwise I'd put you on guard duty  with Surly and Stinker …" Selena's pointed ears pricked up. "Hang on! What's that?"

Emily and Aisha listened too. They could hear faint shouts coming from outside the pillow fort. Slumbertail and Trixie must be fighting the trolls! "I hope they're OK," murmured Aisha in Emily's ear.

Screech made muffled noises through his closed beak.

Selena rolled her eyes. "You may speak, silly owl!"

"Thank you, your nastiness," said Screech. "Shall I go and see what Stinker and Surly are doing?"

"No," snapped Selena. "You must stay here with the locket. I'll go." She stood up and huffed. "It's impossible to find reliable minions these days …"

The girls pressed themselves into the soft walls as Selena stomped past them, kicking pillows out of her way.

"Now's our chance!" whispered Aisha.

The girls peeked into the room again. But Screech wasn't on the floor any more. After a moment, Emily spotted him. She pointed to where he was perched high up

in the wall, nestled between two pillows. The locket still hung from his neck.

"Oh no!" mouthed Aisha. "How are we going to get up there?" She frowned. "The pillow walls will just fall down if we try to climb them. And it's too high to jump …"

Emily gasped. "I know!" she whispered. "Have you still got Hob's potion?"

Aisha's eyes went wide. "The leapy potion! I think I have it somewhere … but where did I put it?" She stuck a hand into her dressing-gown pocket and pulled out the bottle of bright blue potion with a grin. Emily grinned back, and the girls each swallowed a few drops. The potion fizzled on their tongues, filling their mouths with the taste of blueberries and lemons. Then they stepped into the pillow room.

Screech gave a startled squawk. "Not you two again!"

"Hi, Screech," said Aisha. Then she jumped. And she soared up into the air.

This must be how the unicorns feel when they fly! thought Aisha.

She jumped almost as high as Screech, before she fell back down and landed on the soft pillow floor.

"Get lost!" Screech yelled. "Interfering girls!" He flapped to the opposite wall and crammed himself on to a pillow right by the ceiling.

Emily jumped next. She sprang up as if she were on a trampoline, stretching her

arms up towards
the owl.

"Selena!" shrieked
Screech. "Selena,
come back!"

He took off again,
just swooping
through Emily's
hands.

While he was still
flying, Aisha leaped
up again. She
twisted in the air,
aiming just ahead
of Screech, her
hands cupped as if
she were catching

a cricket ball. Screech flew right into her path. He flapped desperately, trying to swerve, but Aisha's fingers closed around the locket. *Click!* The clasp came undone and she pulled it free from Screech's neck.

"No!" yelled Screech. He landed on the pillowed floor in a feathery heap.

Aisha's jump was so big, she carried on soaring, the locket in her hand, and hit the soft ceiling.

The pillows began to wobble. As Aisha landed beside Emily, a pillow fell down. *Ffflump!* Then another fell, and another. *Ffflump! Ffflump!*

"Watch out! The whole fort's collapsing!" cried Emily.

Chapter Eight
Feather Flower Pillow Fight

Screech flapped to avoid being buried in pillows, as an entire wall of the fort toppled around them. Aisha and Emily tried to bounce aside, but the leapy potion had worn off. Batting away the falling pillows with their hands, they scrambled through the collapsing fort and out on to the mountain.

Slumbertail, Trixie and the trolls were fighting – but with pillows, and they were clearly having fun! Surly giggled with delight as a pillow wielded by Slumbertail hit her bottom and burst open, sending up a cloud of Feather Flowers.

"Me next! Hit me!" Stinker cried, hopping about with excitement. Trixie bopped a pillow on his head and he doubled over with laughter.

Selena stamped her hooves beside them, her face as angry as one of her thunderclaps. "Stinker! Surly! Stop that at once!" she ordered them furiously. "Or I'll fire you!"

"We don't care," Surly said gleefully.
"This is much more fun than being your
guards!"

Just as Selena opened her mouth to
reply, Screech shot out of the collapsing
fort. "Your nastiness," he yelled.
"Emergency! It's the girls – they've got
the locket!"

Selena whirled around.

Her eyes flashed as she took in the girls, the locket clutched in Aisha's hand, and the fort collapsing behind them. Lightning crackled from her horn. "How dare you interfere with my plans again!" she snarled. "That locket belongs to me!"

She marched towards them. Aisha and Emily took a wary step back.

"Actually," retorted Slumbertail, "that locket belongs to *me*!"

Before Selena could reach the girls, Slumbertail galloped up to them in a blur of pink. Emily and Aisha scrambled on to her back and Slumbertail sprang up into the night sky, Trixie whizzing along with them. Selena gave a furious whinny, rearing up and kicking her hooves.

"Curses!" Selena shrieked. "You may have won this time, but I've still got one more locket. I *will* be queen of Enchanted Valley!"

"Not while we're around to stop you!" yelled Aisha.

Selena's horn blazed with lightning. Beside her, Surly and Stinker were playing in the collapsed pillow fort, throwing up

armfuls of Feather Flowers and giggling. But all three of them were all already fading from the girls' view, as Slumbertail carried them high into the night sky.

Aisha leaned forwards and fastened the locket back round Slumbertail's neck, where it belonged.

"Sweet sleeps!" cheered Trixie. "Now everyone in Enchanted Valley can have a nice long nap. I can't wait!"

⭐ ⭐

The girls, Slumbertail and Trixie burst into the hall where the unicorns were holding their sleepover. Everyone looked towards them, their faces filled with hope.

Queen Aurora beamed. "Slumbertail is wearing her locket!" she called. "We can all sleep again!"

Cheers rang through the hall. "Hooray for Emily and Aisha!" the unicorns cried. "Thank you, Slumbertail! Well done, Trixie!"

The three Night Sparkle Unicorns cantered up to nuzzle each of them in

turn. "Now we just need to find *my* locket," said Brighteye, a little sadly, "and night-time will be safe from Selena at last."

"We promise we'll help," Emily told her, wrapping her arms around Brighteye's soft neck.

The other sleep pixies, led by Dixie, flew in a fluttering cloud through the window Selena had broken.

"You're just in time!" Slumbertail told them with a smile. She waved her horn. Golden light swirled around it, and her locket glowed. Then all the pixies cheered – their pillowcases were now brimming over with sleepy dust!

Dixie led the pixies away to sprinkle

the dust over Enchanted Valley. Only
Trixie stayed in the hall, and she held her
pillowcase out towards the girls. "Would
you like to be my helpers?" she asked.

Emily and Aisha grinned. "Definitely!"
Emily said.

Trixie poured sleepy dust into their
palms, and Slumbertail flew the girls
around the hall. The unicorns looked up
in delight as Emily and Aisha sprinkled

shimmering dust over them, singing the
lullaby they had learned from Trixie:

"The moon is bright
So say good night,
And now sleep tight
Till morning's light."

As the dust settled over the unicorns,
they began to yawn and snuggle down
among the pillows and blankets. The little
black foal was already snoring softly.

"It's bedtime in Enchanted Valley at
last," said Slumbertail, landing beside
Queen Aurora. "Thanks to you, girls!"

"We're so glad—" began Emily, and
then she yawned too, and so did Aisha.

"It's bedtime for everyone, I think," said
Aurora with a smile.

Trixie gave each of the girls a tiny kiss on the cheek. "Sweet dreams, sweet friends," she said. "I'll make sure the dragons get  some new Feather Flower pillows."

"Thank you, Trixie!" said Emily.

"And please tell Hob that his leapy potion saved the day after all!" added Aisha.

Slumbertail nuzzled them both. "Thank you for everything," she said. "And sleep well!"

"I think we will," said Aisha, then gave another big yawn.

Queen Aurora's horn glowed, and a swirl of rainbow sparkles surrounded the girls. They felt themselves drift up, as light as sleepy dust, and Enchanted Valley melted away. When the sparkles cleared, they were in the Khans' kitchen once more, sitting at the table with their milk and cookies.

"Wow," said Emily. "That was amazing. We'll need to fix our hairdos, though, or your mum might wonder where I got my pink highlights and you got your curls."

"Let's do it first thing in the morning," said Aisha with a laugh. "Right now I'm so—" But she couldn't finish speaking – she was yawning too hard.

The girls put their glasses and plates in the dishwasher, then padded back up the stairs. They snuggled drowsily under their duvets.

"Sleep tight, Emily," Aisha murmured. Her eyes had already drifted closed.

"Sleep tight, Aisha," said Emily softly. "I hope we dream about unicorns …"

The End

Join Emily and Aisha
for another adventure in …

Brighteye and the
Blue Moon
Read on for a sneak peek!

It was bedtime, but Aisha and her best
friend, Emily Turner, weren't ready to
go to sleep just yet. They were sitting
on the floor of Aisha's cosy bedroom in
Enchanted Cottage, playing another
game of cards. Emily had spent the entire
week with Aisha, sleeping over every
night and having a great time.

"Come on, girls," Aisha's mum called
from downstairs. "Time for lights out."

The girls sighed as they abandoned
their game for the night, but climbed into

their beds.

After ten minutes Aisha still felt wide awake. So did Emily. Although the light was off, a golden glow shone even brighter than the silver moon. The girls both gasped with delight. "Our keyrings!" they said together.

Their little crystal keyrings, in the shape of unicorns, were presents from Queen Aurora. She was the wise and friendly unicorn who ruled over Enchanted Valley, a secret magical world where Aisha and Emily had had many adventures together.

When the keyrings glowed like this, it meant Queen Aurora was calling them.

Aisha quietly scrambled out of bed. "Time to go back to Enchanted Valley!"

"I can't wait!" Emily said with glee.

They snatched up their keyrings and pressed them together. A swirling fountain of rainbow sparkles whirled around them, lifting them up off the floor.

Quick as a shooting star, the sparkles began to fade away and their feet settled back down on to lush green grass.

Emily looked around and saw they had landed on the slope of a hill they knew well. Queen Aurora's palace stood before them, a beautiful golden building with eight tall turrets that spiralled like unicorn horns.

Aisha looked up into the dark sky with a sigh. "It's still night in Enchanted Valley! It's been night here for ages now."

"We've got to put a stop to it," Emily sighed. "Once and for all!"

Read
Brighteye and the Blue Moon
to find out what adventures are in store for Aisha and Emily!

Also available

Unicorn Magic

Book Five:

Book Six:

Book Seven:

Book Eight:

Unicorn Magic

Look out for the next book!

Daisy Meadows

Unicorn Magic™

Brighteye & the Blue Moon

From the author of RAINBOW MAGIC

If you like
Unicorn Magic,
you'll love …

Welcome to Animal Ark!

Animal-mad Amelia is sad
about moving house, until she
discovers Animal Ark, where vets look
after all kinds of animals in need.

Join Amelia and her friend Sam for a
brand-new series of animal adventures!